When the World is Full of Friends

Gillian Shields
Illustrated by Anna Currey

BLOOMSBURY
LONDON OXFORD NEW YORK NEW DELHI SYDNEY

When the world
Is ready to play,
Friends are near
If you find a way . . .

Everyone in the Rabbit family loved to play.

Albert loved to run and hop and jump.

He was the fastest and strongest in all the little rabbits' races and games.

Tom liked stories and dressing up best.

He was a
pirate rabbit,

a monster
rabbit

and a marvellous,
magical prince rabbit.

Flossie was a
great inventor.

She loved to play at making things
and painting them bright colours –
windmills and forts and twirly paper umbrellas.

As for the baby, Pipkin, he loved best of all
to play on his blankie by the wide, watery stream,
catching his toes in the sunshine.

So the little rabbits played together,
and they were busy and good.

One day, though, when they were all rather tired,
Flossie said, "I wish we had some friends to play with."
"Friends!" said Albert.
"Friends!" said Tom.
"Ooh!" squeaked Pipkin.

And they knew that they wanted friends
more than anything else in the world.

The very next morning, something tremendous and wonderful happened. A family of squirrels came to live on the other side of the stream, and there were two small squirrels – just the right size to be friends.

The little rabbits and squirrels waved to each other.

"Now we'll have friends
to play with!" cried Flossie.
But it wasn't as simple as that . . .

"How can we get across the wide, watery stream?" asked Albert.
"There isn't a bridge for miles!"

"Oh, bother!" said Tom.
"Ooh!" squeaked Pipkin.
It was so dreadfully disappointing.

But Flossie knew there must be a way.
She sat quietly and tried to work it out.

"I'll think of something, I've got to!"

Then Flossie had an amazing inventing idea. "We'll tie balloons to a basket and fly across the stream," she explained.

Oh dear! The balloons weren't big and airy enough to make the basket fly.

"We could do a hop, skip
and a leap across!" said Albert.
"I don't think so," said Mother Rabbit, kindly.
Even Albert couldn't leap that far.
The little rabbits and squirrels felt so sad.

But Flossie wouldn't give up.
She invented and invented,
until at last she said,
"Albert, you're fast and strong.
Run and find some nice
big pieces of wood and rope."

So Albert did, and when Father Rabbit saw what the little rabbits were trying to make he smiled and came to help . . .

. . . until their brave,
beautiful boat was finished.

"We must dress up!" said Tom.
Soon the little rabbits looked
like daring sailors and pirates,
ready for the voyage.

There was only one more thing they needed.

"A sail," explained Flossie.
"Blankie!" squeaked Pipkin.
And it made the perfect sail!

"Jump aboard, sailors," laughed Father Rabbit.

He steered them safely across the wide, watery stream
to where they could meet the little squirrels at last.

"Hooray!" they all shouted. "Now we can be friends!"
"Hoo-hoo!" squeaked Pipkin.
And Flossie was right . . .

playing with friends
was wonderful!

When the world
Is full of friends,
The fun and laughter
Never ends.